I0654661

Adele A. Gleason

Songs and Verses for Christmas

Adele A. Gleason

Songs and Verses for Christmas

ISBN/EAN: 9783743418561

Manufactured in Europe, USA, Canada, Australia, Japa

Cover: Foto ©Andreas Hilbeck / pixelio.de

Manufactured and distributed by brebook publishing software
(www.brebook.com)

Adele A. Gleason

Songs and Verses for Christmas

SONGS AND VERSES

FOR

CHRISTMAS

BY

ADELE A. GLEASON

BOSTON
CUPPLES AND HURD
The Algonquin Press
1888.

To

MY FATHER,

Whose Daily Life is an Unwritten Poem.

CONTENTS.

	Page
My Father's Kiss	11
The Old Love	12
The New Love	13
The Water Lily	14
My Friend	15
To S. L. C.	16
The Birch Tree	17
The Falling Star	19
The Lighthouse	20
The King's Tears	21
Comrade	23
Not There	24
Butterflies	26
Two Angels	27
An Old Song	28
The Tiger Lily and the Rose	29
The Kiss	31

	Page
White Loves	32
Trillium	33
The Violet	34
Untilled	35
Thy Crown	36
Good Night !	37
At the Gate	38
The White Cloud	39
The Blackened Branch	40
The Storm	41
The Basil Pot	42
Pine Lake	43
Tempted	44
Pardon	46
A Letter	48
Cupid's Song	49
Trust	50
Alone	51
Sealed Orders	53
Thine Eyes	54
August	55
The Captive	56
The Orchard	57

	Page
Bivouac	58
Buddha's Mirror	59
Suspicion	60
Invisible	61
The Buttercup Song	62
Consider the Lily	63
Dawn	65
In Church	66
Autumn Moods. I.	69
Friends	70
Autumn Moods. II.	71
Autumn Moods. III.	72
L'Ami Jean	73
The Astral Body	74
Guilty or not Guilty	75
Parted	76
Grafting	77
Court Martial	78
A Song for a Sweetheart	79
Paradise	80
The Prepared Table	81
An Old Song	82
My Loneliness	83

	Page
Dreams .	84
Gray Hair	86
Crowned .	87
The Will of the Spirit	88
My Prayer	89
To Edith .	90

MY FATHER'S KISS.

First born, the lips have no impress.

Shapeless the clay, no thought inwrought.

Eyes learn the first to look, and then to weep.

But blessed are the lips that keep,

Through life, as seal-mark set in wax,

The half-creative kiss of fatherhood.

No other kiss can fit that mould,

Nor can it break until Death's hold

Break the sealed letter of a life that's writ

From earthly fatherhood to that above !

THE OLD LOVE.

As to the oak trees, all the cruel winter,
The dead leaves hold,
     Frost bitten,
     Storm smitten,
     Snow laden — faithful,
     Till, at the springtime,
     Sweet airs and sunshine
     Come to woo
     Leafage new,
     They silently fall,
     Still as a breath,
     Faithful till death !
So will I go, unreproachful ; for sweeter
Is new love than old.

THE NEW LOVE.

Sing I the new love,

The fresh love,

The fair love,

New as the sunrise

And fair as the dawn.

Pluck now the fresh rose,

The fair rose,

The sweet rose,

For who knows

How soon it may fade?

Sing now the new song,

The gay song,

The bright song,

Sing with the same voice

That once sang the old.

The song is old,
The love is cold,
The story told.

THE WATER LILY.

DID fair Ophelia's dying face
   Sink down among thy level leaves?
Is it the breath of her despair
   Thy pearly petal softly breathes?

Then, growing epitaph, o'er sweet,
   The level water is thy rest,
Thou canst not from it raise thy head, —
   So drooped Ophelia's on her lover's breast.

Thy purity and sweetness mute,
   Thy feeble stem, still speak
That lily maid forlorn, who knew
   Only to die, when hearts did break.

MY FRIEND.

THE pine tree's virtue hath thy soul!
It scorns the winter and the sun's neglect,
And keeps as brave a color for the storm
As any maple that the May can deck,
For June and sunny blue of sky.
Yet is there mourning in its loyal heart,
For what I know not, yet I hear it groan.
What passeth? that it makes a moan?

To S. L. C.

O SWEET, brave eyes, that look straight on
   In destiny's supreme despite,
And carry to the darkest heart,
   Asked or unasked, the holy light
Of love, untouched by care
Of comprehension or return !

Look on, brave eyes, immortal look,
   Unsullied by the world's restraint ;
Not choosing measured looks to dole,
   This one for sinner, and that for saint ;
Alike as flowers that bloom the same
For funeral or for wedding fane.

Seek out thy royal peers — O eyes !
  Nor heed the scoffer's evil thought.
Ye know rewards that still in vain
  Such " meaning glances " *never* bought.
Look on and up, in your own truth,
O eyes that are immortal youth !

THE BIRCH TREE.

As the birch tree, growing taller
  By the running of the stream,
Sends across its darkling bosom,
  From its branch, a silver gleam ; —
So thy presence bright leans o'er me,
  So I feel the silver glow
Of thy brighter face, that, smiling,
  Shines upon me as I go.

And we knew what says the birch tree,
 And we knew what says the stream :
" I will touch you," say its branches ;
 " I am running," says the stream ;
" But I cannot bend me lower ; "
 " And I cannot raise my heart ;"
" Winds that leave me "—
" Drouth of summer "—
 Hold the thirst and wave apart.

When the winds come in the Autumn,
 When the rains flush up the streams,
Down will dip those silver branches
 Where but now their shadow leans.
Then the stream shall rush on faster,
 As it every leaf would steal ; —
Dost thou feel the storm on-coming
 As I now the flood tides feel ?

THE FALLING STAR.

THE thoughts of God that reach the earth
    Are like His stars that fall :
They die before they touch the place
    That is the grave of all.
But when they pass they lead the soul
    To seek their place afar,
To see His stars in fixity,
    And love them where they are.

THE LIGHTHOUSE.

OUT of the storm and the darkness
  To the peace of thy heart would I come,
Into the shine of thy presence,.
  My beautiful light, my sun !

Shine on me, warm me, and light me,
  Let me read my fate in thine eyes, —
My tired, bewildered spirit
  Unto their glory flies.

No ! Like the bird at the window,
  Where the cold glass smites its heart,
Thine eyes are the fatal glory,
  Thy smile plays the cruel part.

THE KING'S TEARS.

THEY say King David, on his throne
Amidst his purple, muffled up his face
And wept.
His armèd men came forth, and drew
Their swords as shelter for his royal form
In tears.
And every slave that bore his mark
Bowed down beneath his feet, nor dared look up
For fear.
And all the maidens that he loved
Did shed hot tears upon their white arms
thrown
Upon the earth.
Then came the magi of the realm
To know by art the monarch's secret pain, —
And failed.

Then did there step from out the ranks
A maiden fairer than them all, who said,
        " 'Tis I.
" They who withstand the king, I know
" Shall surely die.   His royal tears condemn.
        " Tis I."
Then spake the king, his mantle dropped,
" I weep because she is the first I kissed,
        " Nor wise.
" Had she refused me, though a king,
" I would forgive ; but that she kissed and
        loved me not
        " Is death."

COMRADE.

COMRADE, leave me! It is treason
For you but to turn your head
Thus to look on me, the wounded,
Midst the dying and the dead.

Still the banner, never taken,
Floats before my fainting eyes;
Never shaken
Still those battlements arise.

Do not lean o'er me to listen
Tho' I moan a loyal word,
Flash and glisten,
Lifted still, thy broken sword!

This the last word that I utter —

A Dieu, I slowly pray.

Stand and mutter

Adieu, then march away.

NOT THERE.

THE roses on my bosom seem to listen for his
step,

The clock strikes on the passing hour, not
coming! not come yet!

Is it my dress that rustles, or is it the maple
leaves?

Or is it the winded dripping, from out the
rainful eaves?

Faintly " Come," I call; and blush, for no
knock was there !

What is it that keeps me waiting ? I know he
is not there.

Not there beyond the doorway, where my fool-
ish heart will be,

Not there where I see the shadow under the
maple tree.,

Not there, not there, my lover; but **here** in
heart and brain,—

The mystical real presence, never to go again.

BUTTERFLIES.

BUTTERFLIES, butterflies, yellow and crimson,
How do ye mock me in fluttering by.
Seems ye would lure from the fair arm of
Psyche
Even the fabled one with ye to fly.

Butterflies, butterflies, purple and silver,
Chasing the thistledown over the grass.
Kisses of lovers, or sleep dreams of children,
Wandering flowers, ye seem as ye pass.

Tent, Sept. 1st.

TWO ANGELS.

ANGEL of the parting day
  Stay while I pray,
For thy face is royal-bright.
  I fear the night.
I beseech thee, kiss for me
  When thou shalt see,
Dawn's angel ; e'er he come
  His day be won.

AN OLD SONG.

YES, forget me, when we're parted,
    Like a song, or jest, or dream, —
Nay, I would not be too real —
    Say at parting, "It did seem!"

When we meet again, remember
    Just enough to make me dear,
As an old song, that surprises
    The half-listening, willing ear.

If you dream, forbear to tell it,
    So my name in silence wear.
And the meaning of thy dreaming,
    Both alike — we will forbear.

If you dream, forbear to tell it,
    Howe'er sweet the meaning be.
I'm the dream and I the meaning.
    Ah ! thou hast forgotten me.

Tent, Sept., 1885.

THE TIGER LILY AND THE ROSE.

ONCE in a royal garden, its chalice sunlit fire,
    A knightly tiger lily did woo in its desire
A rose that on a trellis near
    Did bloom and blush there, higher !

O faint, fair rose, thy petals drop into that
    lily's heart,
    He knows not that ye die to give — while so
    ye are apart.

Forlorn and leafless hangs the rose
  And full the tiger lily's heart.

And at the dusk his petals, bronze and gold,
  Will proudly close
  Upon the perfumed fading petals of the rose.
And this the love I sing to thee
  Of lily and of rose.

THE KISS.

Yes, I hear thee undenying,
I did kiss thee for love's trying.
Forth the barbed arrow sprang
At the fatal bowstring's twang.
I did kiss, for fond love's trying.
Leave me now, for love is dying.
What can I, though undenying ?

WHITE LOVES.

Upon the snowy Alpine heights the Edelweiss
    doth grow ;

Upon the fervid August floods the water lily
    blow ;

The same white meaning to my soul, from fire
    and from snow.

For Nature hath, like human hearts, its passive
    flowers twain —

One blooms when life is at its flood, and one
    in death's rich pain.

Which shall I take from out thy hand when
    we shall meet again ?

TRILLIUM.

EFFLORESCENCE fair; triune whiteness !

Thou art among the flowers the Sabbath witness.

The Virgin loves thee, for thou bloom'st un-
kissed

Among the other flowers thy perfume missed.

They woo thee not; but softly say,

It is the Sabbath, she hath bloomed to-day.

THE VIOLET.

He took from off my weary heart
　　The faded flowers of love's gone life,
And, freshly blown and royal grown,
　　He gave, the purple violet.

Not the cold gleam of amethyst
　　Salutes me yet : I still may let
Thee give me at our tryst, my friend,
　　One flower, the royal violet.

Thy proud humility well suits
　　Its regal tint, its humble pose.
Ah ! friend, I yield the purple, tho'
　　Thou canst not wear the rose.

UNTILLED.

Two roses, fragrant, wild, and fresh !
Their torn stems pleading for the wayside bush
That bore them, out of stony earth,
Unowned, untilled, —but fairer so for me
Than garden bloom, which hath its price.
Give me naught else ; nor ever tame
An impulse, wild and lawless tho' it be,
To any dexterous service wrought
For promise, not for memory.

THY CROWN.

THY forehead whitens!
Year by year its right
To wear the chaplet
There, where sweats of pain
And work are chrysms
Better than baptismal font hath given,
Has come; I set thereon
The shadeless crown!

GOOD NIGHT!

Oh! what is sadder than to say Good night
To empty air, and feel the blight
Of silence answering to the tone,
And know thereby — I am alone!

Alone! still did I say Good night, dear love!
Through distance lone my poor heart strove
In words that fall upon the empty air —
Good night, dear Ave, good night.

AT THE GATE.

I DREAMED that I lay dying,
    And my lover came to me,
And on my lips and forehead
    Did set his kisses three.

And, while my flying spirit
    Lingered to taste this bliss,
There closed again the gateway
    Between that world and this.

THE WHITE CLOUD.

A CLOUD that never rose from out the sea,

A cloud whose ermined majesty

No swamp nor reptile-breeding pool

Gave birth to. Oh! white scroll,

   That like an alabaster seal

   Marks in the blue a grand appeal

To those that shall be pure in soul!

THE BLACKENED BRANCH.

THE blackened pine tree's dying branch
　　Lies stark across the rising moon.
So stands the tree; the moon shall rise
　　In unmasked glory soon.

So, dark across thy shining life
　　My fate's black arm doth plainly lie.
My fate and I shall stand alone,
　　Thy life shall pass us by.

THE STORM.

As bends the tree in the wind
    Before the rain,
So do I bow, when thou comest,
    In sudden pain.
I know thou comest for love,
    Hopeless again.
To the storm of thy grief I yield.
    Not in disdain
Do I hold to my roots : I repose ;
    I stand the strain.

THE BASIL POT.

So now he hath forgotten all!
'Tis well. I said he must.
I wonder that I wish to take
The dry root from the dust
To see if it is dead, forsooth.
Can my proud heart e'er be
A basil pot in which to nurse
A memory of thee?

PINE LAKE.

BEAM of the golden sun, kiss her gold hair,
Kiss it as I would
Were I but there.
Wind from the beech tree, say some sweet word,
Say it as I would
Were I but heard.
Colors of sunset, catch up her bright smiles,
Reflect them upon me
And count not the miles.
Shine of the mystic moon, creep to her pillow,
Lie there and dream with her,
Would I could also.
Light of her rising star, light her hopes for her,
Light of her setting star,
Take her fear from her.

Strength of a stronger heart, reach low and
    love her,
As doth the word of her
        Friend and her lover.

TEMPTED.

Tempted! Yes; my soul must meet it!
    Would to-morrow need not come!
All the long night I rehearse it, —
    Would to God it need not come!

Calm I am; it is not real;
    Half it seems to me a dream.
When the stated time hath brought it,
    Will the dreaded thing be seen?

Seen as now it glares upon me,
  Tempts me with its eyes and breath,
Calls me to its bosom, saying
  " Love me, tho' I be thy death."

Cease, prophetic voice within me.
  Cursed be the voice ! It crieth,
"That temptation shall o'erthrow thee,
  By its subtilties thou diest."

Rise, my angel ! come and shield me !
  Bare thy sword, my naked breast
Shall receive thy weapon, rather
  Than beneath that shield to rest.

So, no morrow shall awake me.
So, I need not go to meet
That which surely shall o'erthrow me,
Trample me with cruel feet.

———

PÁRDON.

NAY, if thou wilt forgive me,
Do it without a plea!
Let me see how royal thou art
If thou wouldst humble me!
Dost know that the cloak of forgiveness
Is the prophet's seamless garb?
He only leaves it to others
When he goes heavenward.

Wait not for my tears to compel thee.

Thou canst not heal me so.

Before my pitiful penance

Let thy rich forgiveness flow.

So shalt thou gain, while I'm losing

What is wasted if thou delay.

Celebrated, a king with pardon,

Thy coronation day!

A LETTER.

I MISS thee! yet would not recall.

As one who largess from a king receives

And cannot count his treasure; only grieves

To see the royal presence vanish out of sight.

And, when the great-one's gone indeed,

Counts up the sum of blessing with delight,

Nor ever thinks to ask for more.

So hast thou left thy love's and wisdom's store

For me to count alone, nor dare to ask

For thy return.

CUPID'S SONG.

Oh ! I mind me of the kisses

That I've spent for love's brief blisses !

Oh ! I mind me of the smart

When the throbbing lips did part.

O ! I mind me of the art

Used to barb the arrow's dart.

O ! I mind me, in love's mart,

How to match a kiss and heart.

TRUST.

WHAT barrier can I set between us?
What stronghold find wherein to be?
Within what armor, invisible but sure?
Or dare to meet thee with the white flag pure?
I will; alone I'll come to meet the fair,
Not e'en in David's sling a smooth-cut word.

ALONE.

ALONE! The merry dancers laugh to see my
    sad amaze.
" 'Twas turning in the dance, " they cry; "it is
    enough to craze."
" A freak," they say, like my wild self,
To dance alone like some mad elf,
Among them all in pairs.

'Tis gone; and yet I surely felt a form within
    my arms.
I surely felt its floating hair, lithe waist, and all
    its charms.
It stepped with me about the floor,
Its hand in mine a pressure gave, as if the dance
    to check.
And then — it was no more.

Last night I sat upon her grave and called;
    she would not come.

I said, " The cruel dead forget, else could they
    not be dumb."

Nay, I will dance no more to-night; the music
    is a dirge.

Ah! boys, she loved me; no more wine —
    don't urge.

No, I would not forget.

SEALED ORDERS.

I RUN on thine errands, my king,
  Through the fight, and the night, and the
    storm.
Concealed next my heart is the secret — the
    word,
  That at risk of my life must be borne.

I know not the message my king
  Would have sent; but I know it may save
    or may slay.
I bear it in haste, and I bear it with zeal,
  The honor, the trust, is my pay!

THINE EYES.

I READ thine eyes!

.   .   .   .

I know the eager meaning of their glance,
I know their ecstacy, their solemn trance,
I know their longing, and the unshed tear,
I know their keen anxiety, their sudden fear,
I know their pathos dumb, their dead despair,
Their hope pathetic and their weary care,
I know their veilèd passion, and, above
All, I read their secret — love !

AUGUST.

In bitter strength of August heat
  I saw a little brook run dry.
I stopped to count the piteous stones
  Where waves and bubbles once ran high.

The golden-rod and aster tall
  Stand there amid the stones.
The resurrection of the brook
  Shines in their golden tones.

THE CAPTIVE.

I SOMETIMES dream thy head is laid,
  My conqueror, on thy captive's breast,
And which is victor, which is slave,
  I do not ask ; so let it rest.

—

So let it rest, thy captive queen
  Smiles o'er thy bended head to-night,
And asks, " Who is the victor here ?
  And wherefore was the fight ?"

THE ORCHARD.

THE quiet comfort and the still belief thy pres-
ence gives
Is like the strength of orchard trees.
They shelter from the sun and breeze.
They bloom so sweetly, not in idle flowers,
But set their fruit and wait the ripening hours
Of rain or sun or cloud.
So do I find thee all love's seasons through :
for never do
We ask for more or other fruits
Than those the tree's first nature suits.
So wholesome is thy cheer and kindness, friend.
So will I count its store, nor fear the end
Of bloom or fruit or shade.

BIVOUAC.

BIVOUAC! bivouac! calls out the thunder.
   Tented be army and nested be bird !
Deep swim the fishes, and, seeking a shelter,
   Fly on the wild herd !
Madly the grounded arms fight with the light-
   ning !
   Out fly the birds from the storm-stricken tree !
Everything trembles except the fair lilies :
   How peaceful they be !

BUDDHA'S MIRROR.

STRANGE is the Indian worship.
The far away Hindoo, devoted
To rites and symbols fantastic,
Over his head while praying
Holds up a mirror for staying
The image of spirit down coming.
This will he catch by ablutions
Poured meanwhile on the mirror.
Drinking the drops that o'erflow it,
Thus doth he taste the immortal.

Kneeling, I hold up the mirror,
Bend but an instant above it.
Tears will I pour there, and, drinking,
Love shall make me immortal.

SUSPICION.

THE cloud that fades away in blue,
　　Nor stays to guard the dying day,
　　Hath stolen all my heart away
With like suspicion of thy love.

—

The wind, that erst from bending flowers
　　Blew to the east a perfume sweet,
　　Has died, and I, or e'er we meet,
The meaning of thy step will know.

The shadow of a wandering bird
　　Flits o'er the page whereon I read,
　　Effacing records — ah ! I need
Its coaxing wing as well for thine.

INVISIBLE.

I SEE my heart on yonder tree.
  Ah me !
Look if you will, you only see
  On yonder tree,
A bird's nest filled with snow.
  Ah me !

I see my heart on the little brook.
  Ah ! look !
What floats so well on the little brook ?
  Ah ! look !
A dead leaf floats upon the brook.
  Ah ! look !

THE BUTTERCUP SONG.

Thou miser, shy, but brave!

How dost thou hold thy gold in such sure way,

That all the clouding of the darkest day

But lets thee shine the more?

When all the sun goes out,

And leaves the green in heaviness,

The hillsides' and the pastures' evenness

Besodden in dull rain, —

Like gold on gaming tables plain,

Thou shinest wanton for the thieving hand.

CONSIDER THE LILY.

In the burning sun the reapers
  Bind the precious sheaves.
On their toiling hands the thistle
  Blood scars leaves.

Is no wheat without the thistle?
  Is no harvest without tares?
Yet and is the harvest precious;
  Worth all cares.

Oh! ye angels, *strong* and *tender*,
  Faithful shall ye be,
Tho' the harvest wound the white hands
  That shall reap for me.

But the Lord, who sends the angels,
  Comes, and now I see Him stand,
And from out thy field a lily
  Plucks He with His blessed hand.

And I know the vision's meaning —
  That thy field is holy ground;
For He smiles upon the harvest
  Where the lily shall be found.

DAWN.

MARIA, send an angel
  To wake me when 'tis day.
To rouse me at the dawning,
  To waft my dreams away.
With wings like white clouds shining,
  With eyes as full of light,
To bring my soul its dawning,
  To snatch me from the night.
I shrink into the darkness;
  I dread the coming day;
Its toils and its privations
  Come to meet me on the way.
Maria! send an angel
  To wake me when 'tis day.

Rouse me, as if already,
   In the kingdom that is light,
I waked to dwell forever
   Where "there shall be no night.'

IN CHURCH.

WHEN I see him sitting by her
In their godly pew in church,
I remember, I remember
The solemn moonlight's splendor
When he made the great surrender
Of all he had to tender
To one who could not do
What is now so nicely through,

In the blending two in one.

(I can now see how 'tis done.)

But has he ever told her?

Is that why the coldest shoulder

She ever turns toward me,

And so plainly lets me see

That she's the happiest woman,

And he's the happiest one man

That loved her first and last,

That loves her sure and fast?

And I may envy if I will,

And watch, as from a window-sill,

The glory of the woman who

Has known what I have ne'er been
through, —

The proffer of the hand of man,

The bliss that doubtless never can

Come to the likes o' me !

But only this I'd like to see —
My lady come with thanks to me
(And she should very thankful be)
For that one No, that she must know
Has brought her all her bliss below.

—

AUTUMN MOODS. I.

SOMETHING fails from out my heart,
  As the autumn leaf from the winded tree.
Helpless I stand like a bare, bare branch!
  Alas! must the winter be?

The green leaves kept me from too much sun
  They died from his burning kiss.
It smites me now on my branches bare
  Is this the winter? this?

FRIENDS.

SPRING hath wooed the rosy sunrise!
Summer loves the golden noon!
Autumn knows the purple sunset!
But the Winter has the moon!

AUTUMN MOODS. II.

How proudly doth the tree shake off her leaves,
When once they blush beneath the autumn sun,
And clasp the shining beams of light
In arched and quivering branches with delight

As Venus cast from off her rich disguise
Of silken dress and canopy of lace,
When Jove, in golden shower, would give
His last, his mystical embrace!

AUTUMN MOODS. III.

WHAT is the Spring time, and what is the Summer?

What is their joy and their beauty to me?

Give me the burning regrets of the Autumn!

Give me its purple, its crimson-bright tree!

Give me the strength of its slow-dying passion;

Glory of ripening; its heat-scented ground.

Give me the hopeless, the proud, the rich Autumn,

Who haughtily dies when her treasure is found.

L'AMI JEAN.

It cannot be his fingers
  That touched those silent keys,
And brought out that twilight music
  To speak with the evening breeze.
It must have been the sunlight
  That stole through the glorified trees
And played in echo the bird's clear songs
  Upon the trembling leaves.

It must have been the sigh that crept
  From out a lonely heart,
That swept those sweet arpeggios
  Across my listening heart.

It must have been a quiet tear
That melted with the tone,
And made that last pathetic chord
Like one sweet word — my home !

THE ASTRAL BODY.

As scent of flowers through the darkness
    stealing
Is to the soul of beauty more appealing
Than where in hand-grasp even, all revealing
    Of shape and loveliness, they rest.

So comes thy spirit's blessed visitation
Through silent distance, like the invitation
Of music's prelude for the inspiration
    Of sudden flight or song.

GUILTY OR NOT GUILTY.

I DREAMED last night I kissed you;
  A blessed, sinless dream ;
To-day I coldly pass you.—
  Thank heaven ! I did but dream.
Thank heaven ! and yet that kiss,
  That never touched your face,
Hath gone from out my heart
  And left a tear in place.

PARTED.

MILES of land and leagues of sea
Ne'er had parted you and me.
Time's often-setting sun,
Many a fairer one,
Ne'er 'd do what meeting's done —
          Parted us.

With a stilling touch of peace,
And an awed sense of release,
Meet I the eyes that quelled,
Clasp I the hand that held.
Tremble not, since meeting has
          Parted us.

GRAFTING.

WHY didst thou ask me for a kiss?
  Hadst thou no foresight how it then
    would be?
As graft upon the wild thorn-tree
  A different nature would take root in me?

No more to guard the wayside path,
  With thorny pride defend my flowers.
I feel the smooth-stemmed branch that
    towers
  A garden tree ; for fruit — not flowers.

COURT MARTIAL.

WITH bandaged eyes — Love made them fast —
I stand condemned, and wait the shot.
The minutes pass — hast thou forgot
    To give the order — Love ?

I hear the word — it is reprieve.
I snatch the bandage ; look around !
No armèd men to hold the ground, —
    Only the leader — Love.

He gives me back my flag and sword,
And only says — "Condition be, —
You shall not use them against me,
    For I am — Love."

A SONG FOR A SWEETHEART.

SOWING kisses, careless sweetheart!
 Light as thistle down they fly!
Careless sweetheart, in whose garden
 Will be thistles by and by?

Careless sweetheart! that way smiling!
 'Neath whose eyelids, by and by,
Will the tears creep down and make the
 Heart a desert — sigh on sigh!

Careless sweetheart! arms about him —
 Chains they do not seem, and yet,
Some day you will wish to break them —
 He will not forget.

PARADISE.

THE river, going onward,
   Its music seemed to steal
From out the swaying tree-tops,
   That the tender south winds feel.
The shy, sweet grass and mosses
   About our feet in flower!
For birds it is the spring-time
   For us — it is love's hour.

Earth mourns her ancient Paradise.
   But, wherever lovers be,
There flows its magic river,
   There lives its fatal tree.

But when love's lips are parted,
And ere they leave the place,
Thou canst not find the garden —
'Tis gone — there is no trace.

THE PREPARED TABLE.

THEY in whose veins a hopeless love
Hath set its fire
Are like the feasters at a traitor's board —
Where every sweet and cup with which the
    table's stored
Hath poison that doth rankle and make keen
The appetite, and while they die they seem
More greedy yet to eat before they die.

AN OLD SONG.

ONE day Death came a-wooing,
   But I turned him from the door
With the plea (ah! sad undoing)
   For one earthly lover more !

—

But should Death come a-wooing
   On this day to my door, —
I had rather let him in
   Than one earthly lover more.

MY LONELINESS.

My loneliness, it is a temple,
  Beautiful and still and grand,
Where I worship silently
  With lifted hand.

Solemn, but not sad, not wishful,
  There's an altar ; and the fire
Sees the blessed sacrifice
  Of earth's desire.

Blessed peace ! the temple's surety
  From all care or hate or love,
Built of answered prayers, a lodge
  For heaven's Dove.

DREAMS.

WEARILY came I at midnight
    To my chamber all alone,
To the bed on whose white pillow
    A square of moonlight shone.

I lay me down on that pillow
    With a shuddering, lonely sigh,
And out of the sleep that came to me
    The vision wandered by:

It seemed that the cold, white death-bond
    Did calmly hold me there,
And a presence was round about me,
    That I breathed as I breathe the air.

And the voice of one I had loved
  Spoke like the voice of song,
And called my repentant spirit
  To the heart I had left so long:

" Thy faithless will hath perished
  With the death of the dust in thee,
And the spirit that shall be faithful
  Is set from thy body free.

" The love that comes from heaven
  To which thy soul hath flown,
Shall not betray thy dear one
  As thy earth-born heart hath done.

"Thou wert only fit in dying
  To love such an one as I, —
Wait in the heavens for me
  Till I shall also die."

GRAY HAIR.

OLDER! Oh, yes;
  And my hair must grow old,
But one lock will ever be young.
  One lock — shall the secret be told!
The tress that you kissed, love,
  Will never grow old.

Gray-haired! Oh, yes;
  And white-haired some day,

But e'en in my coffin
    One lock brown will stay ;
For the lock that you kissed, love,
    Will never grow gray.

CROWNED.

WHEN princes marry there is interchange of
    priceless gifts ;
And then the throned leads the other up,
That all may see them equal.
So may it be with you this marriage day,
That one already regnant shall make the other
    room upon the throne,
And both shall rule the kingdom of your love,
    and neither serve.

THE WILL OF THE SPIRIT.

SEEK not the audible !
The voice that cries, distrust;
For by the inward ear, those must
Hear what the spirit wills.

Voiceless and wordless comes
The message that shall rule, —
Mightiest in silence is the school
Wherein the spirit learns.

Resist not heaven, when
A greater force than this
Which swings the earth thou must resist.
The spirit's will, obey!

MY PRAYER.

Not a word : in silence holy
Do I pray for thee,
All my heart-strength, tense and life-strong
Thus my prayer shall be.
And the Christ-heart, tender, gracious,
Feels the thrill I lend,
Answers with the gift eternal,
Not with that I send ;
And the love of God, all sacred,
Blots me out ; and so
With a reverent, glad submission
Out of sight I go.

TO EDITH.

EVERY bird must die some morning,
    Die of a shot, in sudden pain,
Die a starveling, or maybe frozen,
    Die in the snow, or the heat, or the rain.
Die as it flies to lands of summer,
    Die as it sits on its loveful nest,
Die when it seeks its mate at spring-time,
    Or when its throatful song is best !

But, alas for the bird that lies in the meadow
    And slowly dies of a broken wing ;
It hath flown the highest and sung the sweetest
    That dies at last from a broken wing.

www.ingramcontent.com/pod-product-compliance
Lightning Source LLC
Chambersburg PA
CBHW020047030726
47499CB00007B/2619